K.I.D.S.

_____Book 1_____

By Aydin Rizqi

Illustration by Milo Polley

Editing by Sarah Lintakoon

Printed in the United States of America

To Armaan,
My best friend.

Books by Aydin Rizqi

1. Ethan Anderson and the Wielders

Author's Note

This book is a remake. I originally wrote "K!D$" in 2020, but now that I look back at it, I realized I could make it better and more enjoyable.

Chapter 1

Sam gulped as he looked at his new school. He stood in front of multiple small cubicles (they weren't actually cubicles. They were more like portables) that stretched a mile away. The main cubicle, the office, had two pencils crossed in an X, which was the logo for Xavier Middle School.

"Hey," a warm hand touched Sam's shoulder. Sam turned around and faced his mother, who was dressed in her doctor clothes. His mother smiled, which comforted Sam.

"It's okay to be nervous. I was nervous when I started seventh grade." his mother, Aleem, said. Sam was not nervous about one thing. He was nervous about multiple things. He and his family had moved to Toronto, Canada due to the Taliban takeover in Afghanistan. Sam and his family managed to flee Afghanistan, but the dark memories were still with them. Sam hoped Canada would be a fresh start for him and his family.

"But I've never even been to school before!" Sam said. "Now, I'm starting at a new school in a new country in the middle of the school year. What if I don't fit in? What if everyone is weirded out by me?"

Aleem gripped her son's shoulders. "You are going to fit in. Want to know why?"

"Why?"

"Because you are different." Aleem brushed his brown hair. "And being different makes you unique. And soon, everyone is going to want to be friends with you."

"You sure?"

"Positive." Aleem smiled before glancing at her watch. "It's 8:00. Go show them what you can do." Sam hugged his mom and turned around to face XMS.

Sam, who had light-brown skin and brown eyes, adjusted his round-shaped glasses, took a deep breath, and walked in.

XMS was a large school. The school had multiple corridors for students to walk through. There were large openings for students and the staff to walk around and eat. On the outside, there was a large field for P.E, and on the inside, there was an array of posters stapled to the wall that focused on different subjects. Some of them were about clubs, school activities, and events, but there were a large number of posters that talked about bullying.

One thing about middle school is that there is a lot of bullying… well, at least that is what Sam heard from the books he read.

Since the bell had not rung yet, a lot of kids were standing around and talking. Multiple kids stared at Sam as he walked past them.

"Sup, nerd." one of the kids said. Sam could tell he was an eighth grader because of his thin (yet noticeable) mustache.

"Hi," Sam said quietly and quickly walked away. He took out his map of the school, unfolded it, and examined it to find where his first class was. He nodded when he found it and continued walking down the corridors.

Suddenly, the bell rang and the students said bye to their friends. Sam looked up and saw a large, gray cinder block tower that loomed over the school. The tower was shaped like a lighthouse and Sam could see a person inside watching everyone. He was unable to see the man's face, but he could tell that he was wearing a well-tailored blue suit.

Sam remembered reading about the tower and how it was used to watch the students as they went to their classrooms. He put his head down and hurried through the crowd of students. He walked to the back of the school where the last set of cubicles were placed and entered Room 47.

. . .

Inside the small cubicle, a large table was placed at the corner of the room where the teacher sat. Sitting in their table groups of four, students were working and talking. The walls were painted white and had

posters about science. On the board was the
question of the day: Do you like burgers?

Sam walked up to the teacher. Ms. Cortez,
whose name was stapled to the wall behind her,
looked up at him. She had blue glasses, red-blond
hair, pale white skin, and when she smiled, Sam
could see the shining braces on her teeth.

"Ah! You must be the new student! Um…"
Ms. Cortez rummaged through the large piles of
paper that were stacked on her desk. After searching
through loads of worksheets, she found Sam's file.
There was not a lot of paper in it, maybe two or
three pages in total. Ms. Cortez opened the file and
after reading through it, she smiled and looked up at
Sam.

"Are you Sameed Afridi?" she asked.

"Yes, but you can call me Sam."

"Well, Sam, I am Ms. Cortez, your science
teacher. It's nice to meet you."

"Nice to meet you too."

"Your table group is the one next to the
door." With that, their conversation ended and Sam
walked to his table group.

When he got there, he studied the students
and the table. The tables were not very interesting.
They had a small opening to keep books and other
things. One of the tables was not occupied by
anyone, so he guessed it was his. One thing about

XMS is that it did not have lockers, so the students had to put everything in their bags or in their table.

However, the students were more interesting. There were two boys and one girl. Sitting next to the table that was not taken was a boy in a green t-shirt with curly black hair, emerald eyes, and black skin. The girl, who sat in front of the unoccupied table, had blond hair with streaks of green and purple and green eyes. She wore fingerless gloves, a blue jacket, a green shirt, and white pants. Sitting next to the girl was a thin boy with curved eyes, soft black hair, and pale skin.

His new table mates were reading something about cells and molecules in their science textbook.

"Hi." Sam said. The thin boy looked up at him.

"Oh-my-god! You must be the new guy!" The boy grinned. "Hi! I'm Dany Li!"

"Nice to meet you, Dany. I'm Sameed Afridi. But you can just call me Sam." Sam could tell that Dany was very upbeat.

"Sameed Afridi? Are you Afghani?" the other boy asked.

"Yes, I am."

"Oh… I'm sorry to hear about… well, you know what is going on in Afghanistan. My home continent, Africa, is going through a lot of things too."

"I'm sorry." Sam said.

"Don't be," the boy shook his head. "It happens. By the way, my name is Idi Bocku." Sam shook Idi's hand.

"Nice to meet you, Idi." He sat down in his seat and set his backpack next to him.

"When did you move to Toronto?" the girl blurted out. It was the first time she had spoken. Sam looked at her with a puzzled expression

"How'd you know I moved here?"

"I just genuinely know something about someone when I meet them… and you are wearing a short-sleeved shirt in Canada in the middle of February… so, yeah. By the way, my name is Kathy Winston. So, you are a refugee?"

"Yeah. I had to leave Afghanistan because of the Taliban. I moved here 5 months ago." Sam nodded, "Nice to meet you." "

"It must be a big change for you." Dany said.

"Yes. Unlike Afghanistan, it's really cold here. Plus, I've never had an education. Everything I know comes from what my parents taught me, what I see or hear, and what I read from books." Sam sighed remembering all the things he had to go through in Afghanistan.

"Wow, that's harsh." Dany blurted out.

"Hey," Idi said. "Don't worry. Here you can start a new life in a new home," Idi put his hand on Sam's shoulder. "With new friends."

Sam looked at his table mates. "Friends?"

"Yeah! After hearing about all that stuff, you are like the coolest person I've ever met." Dany said. Kathy simply nodded.

Tears swelled in Sam's eyes. "Thank you… friends."

Chapter 2

To Sam, the fourth period was particularly interesting. Fourth period was his elective: Boys Self Defense.

Sam had never been a fighter and tried avoiding fights. Out of all the electives, he could have chosen something else, but it wasn't his choice.

He was going to pick Robotics, but his father said "Sam, you are growing up and one day you will be a man. And men need to know how to protect themselves and others. So, I would go for Self Defense."

So, he chose Boys Self Defense (there were two self defense classes: Boys Self Defense and Girls Self Defense) and now he was learning how to fight.

He opened the door to the small gym (there were five gyms in XMS). The small gym was about the size of a one-story house. There were blue and white pads lined against the wall and the floor was covered with black floor pads. One of the walls had a large shelf of weapons. The weapons were like a combination of a long knife and a short sword. Not too big and not too small. The blades were golden and the grips were wrapped in black cloth.

Sam was going to walk toward them but then he heard a sound like a clap. The doors of the gym suddenly swung open as the other students walked in. They were talking among themselves and they all wore black shirts and pants.

They stopped what they were doing and looked at Sam.

"Where'd the nerd come from?" one of the boys said.

"Hey, is that how we talk to new students?" a man walked through the crowd of boys and looked at Sam. "Say sorry, Harley."

"Sorry," Harley said, but he sounded like he didn't mean it. The man, who Sam assumed was the coach, walked toward Sam.

"What's your name, sport?" the man said.

"Sameed Afridi. But you can call me-"

"Sam. I'll call you Sam."

"Yeah." Sam mumbled.

"Well, Sam. My name is Al Alson. You call me Double A or Coach Al."

"I'll go with Coach Al." Coach Al had curly white hair. He was really tall, buff, and he wore black pants and a white shirt.

"Well, because you are new, it's best if my assistant tells you everything." Coach Al turned around and looked at the students, "Blade."

Blade was actually the shortest one in the group of boys. He had black hair that was all over the place as if he just experienced a hurricane. He wore black shorts and a black shirt, he had dark brown skin, and his eyes were slightly curved.

"Hi," Blade said. "I'm Blade Anong. Nice to meet you, Sam."

"Nice to meet you too." Sam said as he looked down at Blade.

"Well," Coach Al clapped his hands, "let's get to work."

Blade seemed to know what to do. He walked toward the large punching pads that were located at the side of the room. Sam followed him.

"So, do you know how to fight?" Blade asked.

"No. I can only throw a weak punch." Sam said bleakly.

"It's okay. I'll help you." Sam stared at Blade for a moment. How could he, a kid the size of a nine-year-old, be able to be a Self Defense Coach's assistant?

"I can tell you are shocked that I am the Coach's assistant even though I am short." Blade said without even looking at Sam.

"Yes. Sorry" Sam apologized.

"It's okay. I get it a lot. The simple answer is that I have not hit my growth spurt yet."

"Ah." Sam nodded.

"But being short helps me. My opponents may be stronger and bigger, but I'm faster." Blade studied Sam. "You're not that tall either." Sam nodded.

"Now, let's see what you've got." Blade gestured toward the punching pad. Sam sighed and punched the pad weakly. Blade shook his head "Come on. I know you can do better than that."

Sam punched the bag again but with a little bit more force this time.

"Harder." Blade said.

Sam punched the pad again.

"Harder," Blade said but more sharply this time.

Sam punched the pad and there was a small thumping noise.

"Harder!"

Sam punched the pad again and there was a larger thump.

"HARDER!"

Sam screamed and he punched the pad so hard that he tore a small hole in it. All the students and the coach were staring at Sam, which caused him to look away in embarrassment.

"Sorry everyone. Just helping Sam here. You can go back to your training." Blade said calmly. The boys nodded and kept training. Blade looked at the hole in the pad then at Sam. "Good."

Then he walked away. Sam gulped nervously. Even though Blade was small, he was a beastly fighter.

Chapter 3

"Oh, yeah. You do not want to mess with Blade."
Idi said. It was lunchtime and the school was
bustling with students. Some were eating, some
were playing games, and others were talking. Sam
and his friends sat on the field and ate their food.

Sam had just told his friends about what
happened in the fourth period.

"He's like a tiny beast who can kill you in a
second!" Dany exclaimed.

"Really?" Sam asked.

"Oh, yeah. He's like Bruce Lee and
Muhammad Ali combined." Kathy said.

"Where is he from?"

"I think he's from Thailand." Dany grinned.
"So, he's a fellow Asian."

"Cool." After that, they ate their food in
silence.
Sam was growing fond of his new school and his
nervousness from the morning had faded away.

"Bullies." Sam blurted out.

"What?" Dany asked, his mouth half full.

"Nothing."

"Something about bullies." Kathy stated.

"Oh!" Idi said, "I forgot to tell him about the
bullies."

"Please don't." Sam begged.

"You need to know."

"The bullies here are like all of the other bullies in the world. They pick on basically everyone." Dany shrugged.

"Oh." Sam whispered.

"There are four bully groups: 360Chinese, the Amakhosi, TickTockGals, and the Emperors." Sam nodded. He recognized the word 'Amakhosi' as 'King' in the African language, Zulu.

"The Emperors are the most feared bully group in the whole entire school." Idi stated. "There are three members: Bill, Nill, and-"

"STEVE XAVIER!" someone screamed. Everybody, except for Sam, gasped as Steve Xavier walked through the field. Everyone went silent as they stared at Steve. Steve was an eighth grader and was quite tall for a 13-year-old. He had curly blond hair, green eyes, and he wore a blue shirt with a small X on it and maroon-colored pants. He was so buff that his muscles stuck out from his shirt. Steve eyed everyone with a threatening glare. Sam was confused.

"Why are we so silent?" he asked. Everyone gasped and Kathy gave him a look that said *You shouldn't have spoken.* Suddenly, Steve grabbed Sam's collar and lifted him into the air. Sam started shaking with fear. Steve studied Sam. "I've never seen you before." His voice was a little deep and sharp.

"I-I'm new." Sam muttered. The bully scoffed.

"New, huh? Well, what a treat." Steve drew Sam closer to him. "I am Steve Xavier, the leader of the most feared bully group in the school: the Emperors!"

"Thank you for that very detailed explanation." Sam said.

"Are you mocking me?" Steve sneered menacingly.

"No," Sam said quickly.

Suddenly, Steve threw Sam five feet away. Steve walked over as Sam adjusted his glasses.

"You seem like a smart kid, am I right?" Sam nodded. "Well, lucky me. You can do my homework for me." He pulled multiple crumbled packets of paper and tossed it to Sam. "By the end of the week, they should be done." Steve walked away.

When Steve exited the field, Sam breathed a sigh of relief. Dany came and helped him stand up.

"Dude, you just got threatened by Steve!" he said.

"Is that a good thing?" Sam asked.

"No! Not at all. If you don't do what he told you, you'll be dead!"

"Thank you for telling him that, Dany." Kathy said sarcastically.

"What? I was just stating the facts."

"Sam," Idi said, "It's only your first day and you've already gotten picked on by Steve Xavier himself."

"Better watch out." Dany said. Kathy rolled her eyes.

"Don't worry. If you just do what he tells you to do, you guys won't be enemies and fight each other." Dany glared at Kathy when she said this.

"What? I'm just stating the facts." she shrugged.

Sam looked at Steve's crumbled homework. He sighed and nodded. He did not want to be enemies with Steve Xavier.

Chapter 4

After his first day of school, Sam took the bus to get home. He was dropped off at the mail house in his neighborhood called the Immigrant and Refugee Homes, which was a cheap neighborhood for… well, immigrants and refugees. From there, Sam walked to his house, which was a small, one-story building with a small lawn and garage.

"Assalamu Alaikum." Sam said as he opened the door. Sam and his family were Muslims, so they said 'Assalamu Alaikum' to greet each other.

"Wasalamualaikum." his father, Abdul Afridi, said as he walked out of his office, which was really a small closet. "How was your first day at school?"

"Good. I made some friends." Sam answered.

"Great! What are their names?"

"Kathy, Idi, and Dany." Abdul looked up, which meant that he was thinking about something.

"K.I.D.S. Kids!" he said as he looked back at his son.

"What?" Sam asked.

"Your name. K for Kathy, I for Idi, D for Dany, and S for Sam. K.I.D.S.!" Sam nodded. "Homework?" Abdul asked.

"Yes."

"Nothing you can't handle." Abdul kissed Sam on the head. Sam's father was very strong and had big hands. Abdul had light-brown skin, a large oval-shaped face, long hair that went down to his shoulders, and a puffy black beard.

Sam went to his room, which was in front of the small kitchen. He closed the door behind him, set his backpack on his small twin bed, took out his books, set them on the table, and started working. After about an hour, he was done with his homework (including Steve's).

Sam then decided to read the book he was currently reading called "Hatchet" by Gary Paulsen. When he was done reading four chapters, Sam was left with nothing to do.

Sam didn't play video games or watch TV that much because he just wasn't into that stuff. He liked to do things in the real world and not in a virtual world. Eventually, he decided to go for a walk in the park.

His sister, Yasmin, walked out of her room with a groggy look.

"Sleeping again?" Sam asked as he put his coat on.

"Yeah." Yasmin yawned. "What were you doing?"

"Homework and reading." Yasmin nodded.

"How was your first day at school?"

"Good. How about yours?"

"It was fine for High School." Yasmin was two years older than Sam. Yasmin went to a school called High. Not High School, just plain High. Weird name for a school.

Sam put on his shoes and opened the front door "Going for a walk."

"K." Yasmin said nonchalantly. Sam walked outside and closed the door behind him.

It was a nice and peaceful afternoon and the sun was setting, which made the sky purple and red. As he walked around the neighborhood, he said hi to his fellow neighbors (even though they didn't know him). Most of the immigrants and refugees had just moved to Canada, so they were still learning English. Sam's English was pretty good, so some people didn't even know he was Afghani.

The cool air flew into Sam's face, which caused his black hair to fly around wildly. When Sam reached the park, he sat down on a bench and watched the little kids smiling and laughing as they played. They were all so happy. Sam smiled. He was happy that even though they were all immigrants and refugees, they could find peace.

"Sam?" a familiar voice suddenly said behind him. He turned around to find Kathy, Idi, and Dany standing behind him.

"Guys!" Sam stood up. "What are you guys doing here?"

"We live here." Idi said.

"You do?" Sam's eyes widened.

"Yeah!"

"Oh wait." Sam said. "You guys are refugees?"

"No, we're immigrants." Kathy said with sadness. She avoided his gaze awkwardly.

"Oh." Sam said.

"I moved here from America during the COVID-19 pandemic."

"I moved here from South Africa." Idi said.

"And I moved here from China." Dany added bleakly.

Sam gasped. "I'm sorry to hear that. It's sad that we all had to leave our homes…but also cool that we're neighbors! No wonder we all became friends so quickly. Because we can relate to each other!"

"Yeah!" Idi said excitedly.

"Well, Kathy, Idi, and I already knew we lived in the same neighborhood, we just didn't know-" Kathy elbowed Dany. "Ow!" he squealed.

"Anyway, it's great to know that we all live in the same neighborhood. Now we can pl-I mean hang out with each other." Kathy stumbled over her words.

Dany gasped dramatically. "Were you going to say p-l-a-y?"

"What's wrong with saying play?" Sam asked. Dany gasped again.

"You can't say that word in middle school. You can only say 'hang out'." Kathy elbowed Dany again and he squealed. "Ow! Why do you keep doing that?"

Kathy rolled her eyes "He's just exaggerating, Sam. Anyway, we should probably go, it's getting late. But we'll see you tomorrow at school."

They all departed. As Sam walked toward his house, he couldn't help but smile. Knowing his new friends lived in the same neighborhood made him feel like he was not alone.

Chapter 5

It had been one week since Sam had arrived at XMS, and Idi was growing fond of his new friend. Now it was the weekend, and Idi had nothing to do.

"Idi! You better clean up your room or else we're going back to lady Africa." his mom, Zuri, called out.

"Why? Is there a problem with Canada?" he replied.

"No…it's just cold. In lady Africa, it's warm and nice, the food is amazing…" Zuri smiled for a moment as she was lost in nostalgia. She quickly snapped out of it and glared at Idi. "Now, clean up your room!"

Idi sighed. "Yes, ma'am." He made his bed, put his dirty clothes in the laundry, and cleaned his desk.

Idi looked up at the posters of planes scattered on the wall. Ever since he was a kid, Idi wanted to be a pilot. He always wanted to fly up into the sky and travel the world. He knew it wouldn't be easy to become a pilot, especially as an immigrant. He took a seat on his bed and sighed.

How can I ever be a pilot? He thought.

Suddenly, his two little brothers, Izaak and Jamal, ran into the room. The twins climbed onto the bed and started jumping up and down. They were both playing with small plane figurines.

"Hello, brother." Izaak said.

"Which bro?" Jamal asked. Izaak pointed at Idi.

"He." Jamal nodded and continued playing.

Even though they were twins, Jamal and Izaak were very different. Jamal liked getting into fights and saying 'bro'. Izaak liked learning and reading.

The twins both had curly hair and brown eyes. They wore the same shirts and slept in the same room. They were four years old and they liked planes, just like their big brother.

"Hey, guys." Idi smiled "Are you having fun?"

"YES!" Izaak screamed playfully.

"Hey, keep it down. Nana is sleeping." Idi whispered.

"Yes, Izaak. Keep it down for Nana." Jamal teased.

"Whatever." Izaak rolled his eyes. "You wanna play Plane?"

"I'm okay."

"Bye bye." As Izaak and Jamal ran out of the room, Jamal's plane fell to the floor. Jamal didn't even notice. Idi picked it up and studied it. Inside, was a small figurine of an African pilot. Idi smiled. "That will be me one day."

Chapter 6

Ever since he was five, Dany always wanted to be fast. He ran every day and every night, but when he was doing laps at school… he was slow.

Tuesday was Mile Day at XMS, so during P.E the students would have to run a mile. During the second period, which was P.E for him, Dany walked onto the track. There were three P.E teachers: Mr. Walski, Mrs. Patel, and Ms. Fiji.

Ms. Fiji was his teacher and luckily for Dany, she was very nice. Mr. Walski's class was located on the other side of the track and Mrs. Patel's class was located at the corner of the track.

"Ok, people. Let's start with some warm-ups. Let me see some jumping jacks and stretches." Ms. Fiji said. All the students started warming up. When everyone was done, they all lined up on the track. "You got 20 minutes, everyone. Now go!"

The teachers blew their whistles at the same time and all the students started running. At first, Dany was in the middle. Then when the other students from class started running, he watched as they passed him. Soon he was in last place.

He groaned "Come on!" He pushed himself and kept running but he was still going slow. When he was done with the four laps, he was exhausted and drenched in sweat.

"Time?" Dany gasped.

"Twenty-five minutes and forty-five seconds." Dany groaned with disappointment and sat on the grass with everyone else. A few moments later, Ms. Fiji looked at her watch. "Ok, everyone, time to go. Class is over."

All the students stood up and headed to the locker rooms to change their clothes. As Dany stood up, Ms. Fiji came up to him.

"Hello, Dany."

"Hi, Ms. Fiji. Is there a problem?"

"Well, Dany, I was looking at your mile times and one thing I have noticed is that you have been getting a time that is above 20 minutes."

Dany sighed. "I'm just slow." Ms. Fiji put her hand on his shoulder, not realizing how sweaty he was. She grimaced, then wiped her hand on her pants.

"Hey, Dany." she said. Dany looked up at her. "Whenever people start running, do you think they are fast? No."

"But I've been running for years!"

"Yes, but it just takes time. You may be slow now, but one day, something great will happen and you are going to be fast. Very fast. Understand?" Dany nodded. "Good. Now, go to the locker room and make sure you put on a lot of deodorant."

Chapter 7

"Come on." Kathy whispered as she carefully attached the wires together. "Come on…"

The wires let out a buzzing sound when they came together. Kathy leapt up in excitement.

"YES!" she screamed triumphantly. In Kathy's hands was an electric water gun that used voice activation.

"Time to test it out." Kathy poured water into the lid of the water gun and then closed it. She went into the backyard and aimed it at a plant. She tapped the microphone that was used to control the gun.

"Activate," She said. "In three, two, one!" The gun exploded in Kathy's hands, causing water and wires to fly everywhere. Kathy stood there speechless and wet with her mouth open in shock. A moment later she groaned.

"COME ON!" She screamed "I can't build a single thing correctly."

She stormed back into her room and closed the door behind her. She changed her clothes and dried off, grumbling to herself the whole time. When she was done, she sat on her bed, drooping with disappointment.

Kathy looked at all of her failed inventions that were piled haphazardly in the trash. Her dream was to be one of the greatest inventors and engineers of all time. She started off building Lego's when she was four, then she got into robotics. She loved building things, but they never worked.

Later that Tuesday afternoon, during dinner, her mother tried to gently talk about Kathy's projects.

"So, Kathy. Any new inventions?" Kathy sighed and shook her head. "Hmm, I saw," her mom, Karen, pointed at their backyard. "that the whole backyard is wet."

"Don't worry, honey." her dad, Ivan, said. "You are going to invent and create a lot of things when you grow up." Kathy only sighed and looked at her soup.

"Hey, Kathy." Ivan said. She looked at her dad. "When you build your inventions," he said while waving his fork around. "Do you believe you can build them?"

Kathy shrugged "I hope I can."

"But do you believe it?"

Kathy pondered this. *Do I?* She asked herself. *I put a lot of effort into it, but do I believe it?*

Kathy looked at her dad and shook her head. Ivan adjusted himself in his seat.

"See, that is the problem. If you don't believe or think you can build something, then it won't work." Kathy nodded solemnly. She knew her father meant well, but she still felt defeated. The family of three ate the rest of their dinner in silence.

. . .

Later that night, Kathy looked at her failed inventions as she lay in bed.

"Believe." She whispered to herself. "Believe…" Then she fell asleep.

Chapter 8

During snack break between the third and fourth period, Sam and his friends were sitting on one of the benches and eating snacks.

Sam looked up at the watchtower. The man in the blue suit that he saw everyday was standing behind the glass with a shadow covering his face.

"Who do you think that guy is?" he asked.

"What?" Dany said through a mouthful of crackers.

"That guy. In the tower." Kathy, Idi, and Dany all looked up at the tower.

"That's Mr. Xavier." Idi said.

"Really?"

"Yeah. His office is also there too." Kathy added.

"Why is he always up there? Can't he watch us from here?" Dany shook his head

"No one really knows why he is up there. Some kids say that he's always up there to send the message that he is the ruler of all he sees." Dany looked out into the distance. "Like God."

"Dany, you are the only one who says that." Kathy stated.

"No!"

"Yes." Dany sighed.

"Yeah…" he said solemnly.

"We-" Before Idi could finish what he was saying, Steve Xavier and two other boys walked up to them. Sam could tell the other two boys were Bill and Nill Billson, the only twins in school. They wore matching black hats, shirts that were too big for them, and pants that sagged on the ground. The Emperors loomed over them like skyscrapers.

"Well, well. If it isn't the…" Steve paused for a moment to think. "Failures." The twins laughed behind him, but Sam and his friends didn't see what was so funny about that.

"You got my homework, Samy?" Xavier asked.

"Still have to get it finished." Sam said quickly.

"Ah, what a shame. My assignments are due tomorrow." Steve leaned in close to them. "If you don't give them to me by tomorrow morning, you are dead."

"I'll get them to you. Don't worry." Sam replied as he shook nervously in his seat. Sam's friends looked at him with concern. Steve scoffed and walked away with the twins following him. Sam sighed in relief but then gulped nervously.

Don't worry. Everything will be fine.

Chapter 9

Everything was not fine. Steve had given Sam loads of homework. When Sam got home, he struggled to carry his backpack because it was stuffed to the brim with books and papers. After closing his bedroom door, Sam placed all of the work onto his desk, creating a large pile of paper.

He sighed and started working. For the next couple of hours, Sam worked, calculated, and studied all at the same time.

When Sam placed the next piece of Steve's homework in front of him, he spotted something interesting.

"Huh." Sam said to himself as he looked at the paper. "Steve has Ms. Cortez for 4th period science." Sam quickly dismissed this thought and proceeded to fill out the paper.

When Sam was finally done with all of Steve's homework, he was called to dinner. Due to hours of sitting, when Sam stood up his back cracked.

He walked outside and sat with his family at the small dining table. Dinner was kabobs, chicken, rice, and Bolani. Sam put a small amount of everything into his plate and started eating.

Yasmin came to the table with her phone in her hand. She wore a black sweatshirt with the name HIGH on it. Her golden-brown hair flowed down to her elbows. She wore black sweatpants and white socks.

"Where have you been all day?" she asked as she sat down.

"Doing homework." he answered.

"Sameed," Abdul interjected, "Why do you have so much homework today? When you came home, all these papers were flying out of your bag. I thought your school didn't give a lot of homework to new students."

"They don't." Sam answered as he took a bite of his food.

"So why do you have so much homework?" His family all looked at Sam with curiosity, hungry for an answer… and food. He knew he couldn't say what Steve was making him do, so he told his family the truth and a lie.

Truth: "Well, there are two reasons I have so much homework. The first being that..uh…you see, I am doing so well in all my classes that my teachers are giving me work for top students."

Aleem smiled upon hearing this. "Wow! You're doing so good! And the other reason?"

Lie: "Um… so there is this kid in my class whose name is—uh… Justin Brainfart."

"Justin Brainfart?" Yasmin said in disbelief. Sam nodded.

"His last name actually makes sense. Turns out, his family has this issue where their brain cannot function properly. So, he wasn't feeling very good today and he asked me if I could do his homework for him."

Aleem's smile grew. "Aw, I am so happy you are doing good in school and helping others."

Sam feigned a smile and they all resumed eating. As he finished his dinner, his smile melted from his face.

After dinner, he went back to his room to work. Because his work was for top students, it was much harder. And a lot of them had to do with Pi.

What is the square root of Pi?

What are the first 20 digits of Pi?

Is Pi an actual pie?

By ten PM, he was exhausted from all the work he had finished. He dropped onto his bed and immediately fell into a deep sleep.

Chapter 10

The next morning at XMS, Sam handed Steve his homework. Steve checked it to make sure it was all completed, then he grinned.

"Good. I'll spare you." Steve walked away and as he passed other kids, they all stepped back in fear. Sam shook his head and went to first period science.

He sat down at his table with his friends and he sighed.

"Sam, are you okay? You looked annoyed or mad about something." Idi asked.

"Not something, someone." He looked at his friends "Someone has to put an end to all these bullies. Do you know how much work I had to do last night?"

"No." Dany admitted.

"Triple the work I usually do!" Sam exclaimed. Kathy nodded in agreement.

"I feel bad for you, Sam. You shouldn't be the one doing all that, especially because you are new. You should have just let one of us do it."

"Not me, though." Dany stated. Idi and Kathy rolled their eyes.

"It's okay, guys." Sam said, but it was clearly not okay.

"Hey, look on the bright side. Because you are doing triple the work, you are going to grow up into someone amazing! And Steve will probably be a homeless person." Dany smiled. Sam smiled a little. Dany might not be the smartest or fastest, but he was always there for him.

"Thanks, Dany."

Ms. Cortez stood in front of the whiteboard and clapped her hands to get everyone's attention.

"Good morning, class. Today's Thursday morning is going to be a fun one! Wanna know why?"

"Sure," some of the students said.

"No," another student said.

"Well, today we are having a meditating lesson!" The room stayed quiet.

"And why are we having a meditating lesson?" one of the students asked.

"It's simple. Students in middle school feel a lot of pressure and anxiety. And the best way to calm yourself down is by meditating... I think." Ms. Cortez said with some confusion. "Anyway, I would like to welcome the meditating master himself, Old Man!"

Suddenly, a very old man jumped out of nowhere and appeared next to Ms. Cortez. The man was extremely old, as his name suggested, and the only thing he wore was a loin cloth. He had a long white beard, a bald head, and dark skin.

"Namaste, pupils." Old Man put his palms together and bowed.

"Hi." most of all the kids said.

"Mr. Old Man has decided to help students in only my classes. No one else's. Can we say thank you to Mr. Old Man?"

"We're not babies, Mom!" someone screamed in the back. Most of the students, except for Idi, Kathy, and Sam, snickered. Dany let out a slight laugh.

"I'll take it from here, Ms. Cortez." Old Man said politely.

"Great," Ms. Cortez walked back to her desk.

"Well, my pupils. Today we are going to do a special type of meditation called Rushils." Sam's eyebrows furrowed with concentration and confusion. Rushils? He had never heard that before.

"I know that most of you don't have any interest in meditating, so I know for a fact that you do not know what Rushils are. Well, my young pupils, I do." Old Man smiled. "Rushils can do different things to a person. It can help people mentally and spiritually, it can mutate you, but that rarely happens, and it can even give you special abilities." Old Man looked at Sam when he said this before quickly looking back to the class. "So, who is ready?" Every student raised their hands.

"Good. Now, do as I say." Old Man took a deep breath. "Close your eyes and sit up straight." The students did as they were told. "Look deep inside yourself. What do you most desire? Who do you want to be?"

Sam looked deep inside. He had never really known what he wanted to be or do. Then he thought about the Emperors.

I want to be able to stand up and protect myself. An image appeared in his mind: he saw himself taking down the Emperors on a plane that was about to crash. He saw himself fighting people in suits on a highway. He saw himself fighting a large machine. He saw a fighter. He saw a… protector.

"Open your eyes." Old Man ordered. Sam and everyone else in their room opened their eyes, which were glowing like spotlights in a stadium. Sam felt power and strength flow through him. Something he had never felt before, and he loved it.

Then the surge of power disappeared, leaving Sam weak again. He suddenly grew very tired and was about to fall asleep, but he stayed awake.

He looked at Kathy and Idi, who were both awake but were groggy and tired.

"Are you guys tired?" Sam asked quietly.

"Yes." Kathy yawned.

"Tired? Yes. But Dany is asleep." Idi pointed at Dany, whose head was drooping.

"Dany," Kathy shook him. This caused Dany's face to fall onto the desk with a THUD.

"Well, he is out." Idi yawned.

Sam looked for Old Man, but he was gone.

Chapter 11

After first period, Sam, his friends, and all the other students were very tired. During snack time, he and his friends sat on a bench, but they were too tired to eat their snacks.

Kathy yawned. "Why are we so tired?"

"I don't know." Idi mumbled.

"Well, I did go to sleep a little late last night. Maybe that's why." said Sam.

"Well, that may be true for you. Not for us, though."

"Dany is doing the worst out of all of us." Kathy pointed at Dany, who was sleepwalking haphazardly. They watched as he walked into a wall and woke himself up.

"What happened?" he yawned briefly before he drifted back to sleep and continued sleepwalking. The routine went on: sleepwalk into a wall, wake up, say "What happened?", fall back to sleep, and repeat.

"Isn't it kind of strange that before the first period we were not tired but after..." Kathy trailed off into a yawn.

"What do you mean?" Sam asked.

"I have a feeling this has something to do with the Rushils."

"Maybe." Sam shrugged.

"True." Idi sighed "Well, it's almost time for fourth period. We better go." He stood up and slowly walked away. Kathy did the same. Sam walked up to Dany and tapped him on the shoulder.

"What happened?" Dany said groggily. "Oh, Sam."

"We gotta go." Sam handed Dany his backpack. "Here."

"Thanks." Dany grabbed his bag and almost dropped it. He gave a small smile and walked away.

As Sam yawned, he caught sight of his reflection in a puddle of water. He looked like he was ready to pass out.

Maybe it was the Rushils.

. . .

By the end of the day, Sam noticed that every single student who had Ms. Cortez as a teacher was tired. Even the Emperors were tired to the point that they didn't look as frightening as usual.

When the bus dropped Sam off at the mail house, he was too tired to walk. It took him nearly an hour to get home.

"Hi." Sam mumbled as he entered the house. "Sam! How was—Oh, are you okay? You look tired." Abdul asked.

"Just a long day at school. I'm gonna take a nap." Sam trudged into his room.

"Okay. You get some rest. Don't be late for dinner!"

"I won't." Sam dropped his bag on the floor and closed his door. The world around him seemed to be twisting and turning, which caused him to become extremely dizzy. He set his glasses on the nightstand and fell onto his twin bed.

Suddenly, it felt like all the air in the room had been sucked away. He gasped and clawed at the air like he was trying to grab the oxygen. His throat became extremely dry.

The lack of oxygen caused Sam to fall into deep, deep sleep.

Chapter 12

When Sam woke up, he was lying in his bed which was drenched with his sweat. Everything was blurry and his ears were loudly ringing. He lay on the wet bed for a few more minutes until he came to his senses.

When he did, he stood up and stretched. He reached for his glasses but when he grabbed them, they broke in his hand. Sam held the broken pieces of his glasses in his hands, confused.

How am I supposed to get this repaired? He wondered.

He suddenly realized that he actually didn't need his glasses. For some reason, everything was perfectly clear. He even saw a small fly on the other side of his room.

Why do I have such sharp eyesight?

He noticed that his shirt was so tight that it was basically choking him. He looked down and saw that his pants were torn and no longer fit him.

Why do my pants not fit me anymore?

As he moved his legs, his pants tore off. He tugged at his shirt to remove it and it ripped open. Confused, he walked awkwardly to the bathroom and studied himself.

Sam grabbed the faucet, but it broke off in his hand. He stared at the broken faucet in shock before gently setting it to the side. He tried to take off his underwear, but it was so tight that it wouldn't budge. Sam grabbed the glass shower door.

Suddenly, all the glass broke and fell onto him, which caused him to have multiple cuts. Sam winced in pain as he stepped on the broken glass to get inside his small shower. He grabbed the shower hose, raised his foot, and plucked the shards of glass out. When they were all out, the cuts suddenly disappeared. Before he could process this, the shower hose broke and Sam fell onto his back. Cold water rained down on him.

A moment later, the shower and all the lights turned off. Sam spat water out of his mouth and stood up in the darkness.

Yasmin walked into the room "Sam, you are gonna be late for–Why is it so dark in here?" She turned on the light and her eyes widened when she saw Sam, although she wasn't sure if it was really Sam. The Sam she knew was nerdy and not strong at all, but this Sam was very muscular. Sam had long arms that were bulging with muscles. His chest bulged out with even more muscle.

"What the-?" Yasmin gasped.

"It's puberty." Sam said quickly.

"Okay." Yasmin said slowly as she backed away awkwardly. She finally walked out of the room and Sam sighed in relief.

I need to tell the others.

Chapter 13

During snack break, Sam learned that Kathy, Idi, and Dany were going through the same thing as Sam.

"Maybe it's puberty?" Dany suggested.

"I doubt it." Kathy said.

"I agree. Puberty doesn't make you control the air." said Idi.

"What?" Kathy, Dany, and Sam said in unison.

"I'm as confused as you! When I woke up, I had placed my hand on my bookshelf, but like you guys, it broke under my strength. All my books were about to fall until suddenly they were floating in the air with the wind flowing around them."

"Woah!" Dany said.

"Keep it down." Kathy hushed him, "Something similar happened to me too. I was working on my latest invention and I didn't have the specific piece that I needed. But when I thought about it, the piece somehow appeared in my hand."

"So, Idi has spooky wind powers and Kathy can make things appear when she thinks about it." Dany noted. "What about Sam and I? Nothing super crazy has happened to us."

"That's about to change." someone said behind him. They all turned around to find the Emperors standing behind him.

"What do you want, Steve? I already did your homework." Sam growled.

"True, you did do my homework. And my teachers were impressed." Steve said calmly. "But you wanna know what happened next?"

"What?" Dany's curiosity took over.

"THEY ALL GAVE ME AN F! BECAUSE THEY KNEW THAT I HADN'T DONE THE WORK MYSELF!" Steve barked. "AND NOW MY GRADES ARE DOWN AND MY FATHER IS DISAPPOINTED!" Steve pointed at Sam with rage. "And it is all your fault."

"What are you going to do to me?" Sam tried to hide the fear in his voice. Steve laughed, which sounded like a lion roaring.

"Not only you! I am so mad that I'm going to take down all of you."

"How are you gonna do that? Gonna bore us to death?" Dany mocked.

"No, worse. You see, we woke up with a little present today." Bill and Nill stepped forward. Nill's hands started generating electricity. Bill's hand glowed with magma.

"Ah, guys." Idi said nervously "I think they got what we have too."

"What do we have?!" Dany cried. Steve smirked as his hand became gooey like slime. His hand morphed into a blade. Dany's eyes widened. "Holy god! His hand just turned into a blade!"

Steve laughed. "Yes! And I love it! Now," Steve glared at the four kids. "Kill them."

"Run!" Kathy screamed. Dany had already started running for his life. Nill chased after him. Kathy and Idi started running in the other direction with Bill following them.

Sam and Steve were still standing there. Steve's hand-blade shimmered in the sunlight.

"You are alone, Afridi. Give up." Steve said. Sam wanted to. He wanted to submit to Steve and let him punish him, but something held him back. Something told him that he did not have to submit to Steve. Something told him he could stand up for himself.

Sam glared at Steve. "Why would I give up when we haven't even started?" Sam said before he took off running.

Meanwhile, Dany was running for his life. "Help me! There is a crazy kid with lighting fingers trying to kill me" he screamed.

"You're the crazy one, kid." said one of the students as he ran past them.

"And slow," another added. Dany looked over his shoulder and saw Nill pushing through the crowd. He shrieked and climbed up the fence, then jumped onto the roof of the cubicles.

He began running, but a bolt of electricity smashed into the roof of the cubicle and Dany fell.

Nill loomed over him and grinned. "You really thought you could outrun me? You're the slowest kid in the school!" Nill pointed his finger, which glowed with electricity, at Dany.

"It's over, kid. You were born slow and you will die slow."

Dany wanted to surrender. He wanted to admit that he was slow. Then he remembered what Ms. Fiji said: You may be slow now but one day, something great will happen and you are going to be fast. Very fast.

Dany felt power surge through him, especially in his legs. He looked up at Nill with shining gray eyes. "Do it."

Nill smirked. Electricity blasted out of his finger, creating a large hole, revealing the classroom inside. Nill blew on his finger and turned around, but then he stopped. Standing in front of him was Dany.

"What? I-I shot you!"

"Did you, though?"

Nill frowned and blasted at Dany again. There was a flash of silver and then Dany was gone. Nill turned around and found the 12-year-old boy was alive.

"How?!" Nill barked.

"I think I found out my abilities." Dany glared at Nill. "Super-speed."

He suddenly shot toward Nill, grabbed him, and carried Nill through school at the speed of light. As Dany carried Nill and ran across the school in seconds, he smiled. He was finally fast. Very fast. He was the fastest kid in the world!

He zoomed past buildings and cubicles. He was running so quickly that whenever he passed a student, they only saw a gray line zoom through the air. Dany laughed with triumph.

. . .

While Dany was running around the school, Kathy and Idi were being chased by Bill who was throwing balls of magma at them.

"Magma!" Idi screamed in fury. "Why magma?!"

"Look out!" Kathy pushed Idi away as a ball of magma flew past them. Suddenly, Bill jumped in front of them with glowing red eyes. Kathy and Idi halted to a stop. Bill shot his arms toward them and a blast of magma flew at them.

Kathy's mind raced as she thought about getting a barrier or some sort of shield to protect them. Suddenly, a large purple barrier formed in front of them and the magma hit the barrier.

"Wow! You really can make anything with your mind!" Idi said.

"I know. It's really cool and freaky at the same time." The barrier disappeared and Bill lunged toward them. His arms were covered with magma and he tried to punch Kathy. She quickly moved out of the way but tripped and fell. Bill raised his fist but before he could smash Kathy, Idi flicked his hands and a wave of wind pushed Bill to the side.

"Don't touch her." he snarled as the wind swirled around him. Kathy's eyes widened.

"Idi, remember what we learned in science class? About magma?" Idi's eyes widened too when he realized what Kathy was talking about.

"Oh yeah!"

As Bill charged toward him, Idi blasted Bill with loads of wind. Bill struggled to stand up as the large amount of wind kept pushing him. Idi stopped blasting him and Kathy kicked Bill in the groin. Bill groaned and he looked at his arms which were covered with dried magma.

"How?!" he cried.

"Science, bro. When magma is cooled, it dries and hardens." Idi and Kathy fist bumped each other to celebrate their accomplishment.

. . .

Sam jumped from cubicle to cubicle with Steve at his heels. During the chase, both of Steve's hands turned into long blades. Steve screamed as he tried to stab Sam, who dodged the attack.

"It doesn't have to be this way, Steve!" Sam jumped to the other cubicle. "We can work something out!"

"I want you dead. Period." Steve jumped over and swung his hand-blades as he tried to chop Sam in half. Sam dodged the attacks again. Infuriated, Steve grunted and one of his hand-blades shifted into a hammer.

"What?" Sam asked in surprise before he was hit by the bulky hammer-hand. He sailed over multiple cubicles and crashed onto one of the roofs.

Steve walked up to him. "Time's up, Afridi. You are not a fighter." Steve laughed.

Sam shook with anger as he glared up at Steve. "Wrong."

Sam lashed out at Steve. He kicked Steve in the chest and then in the face. Steve stumbled backwards, stunned. He screamed with rage and charged. He swung his hand-blades, but Sam blocked all of them with his palms as he sidestepped and elbowed Steve in the chest.

Steve's blades shifted into a long, curved blade. He raised it in the air and was about to kill Sam, but Sam quickly moved out of the way. The curved blade sliced through the roof of the cubicle.

Sam grabbed Steve's bulky arm and wrapped his legs around Steve's hand. He pulled hard and they both fell to the side. Sam jumped off Steve, who crashed face first onto the turf, and landed next to his friends who were already standing there.

"Guess what? I have super-speed!" Dany stated.

All the Emperors who had been taken down stood up.

"So, you all have fancy abilities too." Steve pointed out. "More fun for us." Bill's arms glowed with magma, Nill's hands flickered with electricity, and Steve's hand-blades re-formed.

Wind swirled around Idi, Kathy summoned a large shining sword, Dany stood in a running stance, and Sam had his fists up.
Ready to fight.

The two groups were about to charge toward each other when a large group of teachers interrupted.

"Bill, Nill, and Steve! What is going on?!" one of the teachers said in a British accent. Any proof of their new abilities faded away, and the Emperors acted like they knew nothing.

"I don't know what is going on. Why don't you tell me?" said Steve innocently.

"Kids around the school are reporting to us that you three have been chasing kids on top of the cubicles and destroying our classrooms." said a male teacher.

"Your father is going to be very disappointed," said another teacher. At the mention of his father, Steve frowned and the Emperors walked away with the teachers.

When they were gone, Idi sighed. "That was… interesting."

"Interesting? I have super-speed! It's more than interesting. It's amazing!" Dany cried. Kathy, Idi, and Dany broke into a conversation about their powers.

Meanwhile, Sam stood there in silence, deep in thought. Kathy noticed and she went up to him.

"Sam? You okay?"

"I think I know what's going on with us," he said. "Follow me." Sam ran off and his friends followed. A while later, they walked up the ramp of the school library.

"The library? I haven't been here in a month." Dany stated as they entered. Sam found the shelf he was looking for and he started picking out comics.

"Sam, what is going on? Why are we here?" Idi asked. Sam placed the comics onto the table. Kathy inspected the comics. "Superhero comics? Why are these so important?"

"Don't you guys see? In almost every single superhero comic book, the main character starts off as a normal person who doesn't always get what they want. But one day, something happens to them that changes their life forever." He looked at his friends. "The exact same thing happened to us."

Dany's eyes widened. "Are you saying-?"

"Yes," Sam interrupted, "we have powers.

Chapter 14

Before Idi, Kathy, and Dany could process any of
this, the bell rang.

Kathy shook her head. "We gotta go. But we
can talk about this at the park." The boys nodded
and they all departed.

Sam changed into his Self Defense clothes
in the second locker room (there were at least four
locker rooms in the school) where all the other
students were changing. When they were all done
changing, Coach Al led them to the small gym.
They went inside, did their warmups, and then they
started training.

Because Sam had only been at the school for
two weeks, he was still training with Blade.

"Ok, so today, we are going to work on
moving around and your kicks." Blade said.
Sam was about to nod but then he had an idea.

"Actually, Blade, I would like to do
something else today. Something more advanced."
Sam said.

"You're not ready."

"Try me."

Blade stared at Sam then he lashed out. He
jumped in the air and was about to kick Sam in the
face, but Sam blocked the attack with his palm.
Blade landed and tried to backhand Sam, but he

blocked the attack with his forearm. He grabbed Blade's wrist, spun around, and pulled Blade over his shoulder. Blade fell onto the floor with a loud thud.

Blade tried to swipe Sam's leg, but Sam jumped into the air. Blade started punching and kicking at Sam, but Sam quickly blocked the attacks. He swiped Blade's arms away and he kicked him in the chest.

Blade flew back and he crashed into the wall pad. He was about to get up, but Sam spun around and kicked him in the face. Blade groaned and fell on the floor. All the other students clapped.

"Wow, Sam. Where did you learn to fight like that?" Coach Al asked.

"I... I watch a lot of action movies." Sam answered.

Coach Al laughed. "Ah, reminds me of me when I was younger. Come here." Sam followed Coach Al to the weapons shelf where the strange looking blades were placed.
The coach grabbed one of the blades and showed it to him.

"This is a cyberblade. Archaeologists say that these were built thousands of years ago by a civilization that had declined. But these blades were remade and given to Mr. Xavier after he bought them." Coach Al gripped the cyberblade firmly. "These blades are meant to be used with power."

Coach Al put the cyberblade back in its place and looked at Sam. "Now, show me what else you can do."

Sam smiled and continued showing off his new skills. As he did so, Blade glared at him from the sidelines and thought.

He has taken my place.

Chapter 15

Later that evening, Sam met up with his friends at the park. They sat down on the grassy field where little kids were playing games.

"So, you're saying that because of the Rushils we now have powers?" Idi asked.

"Yes, that's the only explanation." Sam said.

"So, what are our powers?" Kathy asked, looking at her hands.

"Well, from what you guys told me, Kathy can form anything if she just thinks about it. Idi has the power to control the wind and air, Dany has super-speed, and I have... I guess I have martial arts powers."

"How do you know?"

"Because I was able to take down Steve and Blade today. Before today, I barely knew how to fight."

"I have to admit, that's pretty cool." said Idi.

"Thanks." Sam smiled, then he sighed. "Steve is going to try to attack us again." Idi and Kathy nodded. They were still a little shocked that they had powers, but it could make things easier. If Idi got used to his powers and started controlling it, he would be able to fly in no time. Kathy would be able to invent anything. All she would have to do is think about it.

"But we have powers! We can protect ourselves and more!" said Dany, who was the most excited about his powers. After so many years of being slow, he was finally fast.

"Yes, but we have to hide our powers."

Dany frowned. "But I'm finally fast! I-"

"Dany, you can be fast just not too fast… not at school. But outside of school you can run as fast as you want." Sam said. Dany smiled at this.

Sam took a deep breath. He was happy he was finally able to fight and protect himself and others but… did he really want this? Would it be better to stay like this or go back to being his nerdy and weak self? He wasn't sure.

"Well, it's been a long day. We should get some rest." Kathy suggested.

"Yeah." Sam said quietly. They all stood up, said goodbye to each other, and departed.

• • •

When Sam got home, his parents were already there. Aleem was watching the news on the small TV screen and she looked up at Sam and smiled.

"Sam, how are you, my baby?" she asked.

"Good." Aleem studied him and her eyebrows furrowed.

"You look taller." She stood up and gasped. "Oh my, you are nearly taller than me."

"Oh yeah. Sam's been working out."
Yasmin said as she walked out of her room.

"At school." Sam clarified.

"Well, good job. Your father will be proud."
Aleem said.

"I am proud... and surprised." Abdul, who
was in the living room, walked toward Sam. "You
look like me when I was younger. Strong,
confident, and—Wait, where are your glasses?"

"They broke. But I can see without them.
Actually, I can see perfectly."

"Oh... ok. Well, good then. Now we don't
have to pay for them anymore. Well, go get some
rest. And this time come for dinner, will you? Last
night you passed out."

"I will." Sam closed the door to his room
and sat on his bed. He closed his eyes and
remembered the visions he had seen during the
Rushils.

Steve was going to do something that would
put his friends and a lot of other people in danger
and Sam had to stop him.

Chapter 16

During the weekend, Sam and his friends decided that they should start working on getting used to their powers. They needed to do it privately, so they decided to practice at the abandoned park that was about seven blocks away from their neighborhood. In order to do this, they had to lie to their parents.

Sam said that he was going on a walk with his friends, which was partially true because they had to walk to the abandoned park.

Kathy and Idi said the same thing. Dany was about to tell his parents what they were doing, but he caught himself and said the same thing his friends did. After that, they all met at the front of their neighborhood.

Dany wanted to run to the park so it would be faster for him, but Idi said that they should all stick together. Then they were off.

It wasn't a long walk to get to the park. The park was guarded by a large fence, but Idi used his air powers to lift them over the fence and land on the other side.

The park was quite spooky. The playground was rusted and old, some of the trees were dead, and the grass was covered with layers of frost. The only light was the afternoon sunlight.

"Ok," Kathy said as they walked onto the field. "Let's start. So, we all know what our powers are, correct? Anyway, I think I have a way to help us."

"What?" Dany asked.

"Well, because I can form anything if I just think about it, maybe I can make something that will challenge all of us. Like I can make someone who is as fast as Dany and they can race."

"Cool!" Dany exclaimed.

"But won't that take up a lot of your energy?" Sam asked.

"Probably." Kathy brushed a lock of blonde hair from her face. "But it'll be worth it." The boys nodded in agreement.

Kathy took a deep breath and closed her eyes. She started thinking about a boy who matched Dany's speed.

In front of the boys, a figure started to form. It kept growing and growing until it was completely formed.

Kathy gasped and opened her eyes. Standing in front of her was another version of Dany that had blond hair instead black hair.

"Woah! Another me!"

"Dany 1." Sam pointed at regular Dany. "Dany 2." He pointed at the other Dany.

"Race you." said Dany 1. The two Dany's started running around the field so quickly that all

Sam, Idi, and Kathy saw was a trail of gray that they left behind. Kathy then thought of a boy who controlled the wind and a boy who had crazy martial arts powers. Soon, Sam was fighting Sam 2 and Idi was fighting Idi 2.

"My turn." Kathy said and she started thinking about someone who could make anything with their mind.

• • •

Dany 1 jumped over a large branch that lay on the floor. Dany 2 took advantage of this and ran faster. The other Dany tried to keep up.

"I'm not going to let you beat me." Dany 1 said.

"I'm faster either way." Dany 2's voice was deep and distorted.

"Ugh." Dany said in disgust. "What's wrong with your voice?"

"Let's make this a bit more challenging." Dany 2 said. "You see that tree over there?"

"Yes." Dany looked at the dead tree that was on the other side of the field.

"Whoever makes it first is the fastest." Dany 2 suddenly turned sharply and started running toward the tree. Dany 1 tried to do the same, but he tripped and fell.

"No!" He got up and ran after Dany 2. Dany 2 drew closer and closer to the tree with every step. *There is no way I will be able to make it,* Dany thought. Then he saw the playground that was right in front of the tree.

Dany took advantage of this and sped after Dany 2. He got to the playground and jumped off each of the structures. He grabbed the monkey bar and was about to swing over when the bar broke off and Dany 2 fell hard on his back. Dany 1 ran past him and reached the tree.

"I'm the fastest! And always will be!" Dany 1 cried out.

"Great job." Dany 2 murmured as he disappeared into nothing.

• • •

Idi 1 blasted Idi 2 with a gush of air. Idi 2 flew into the air and softly landed on a patch of grass. He swung his arms around, making a whirlpool of air circle around Idi 1, who was suddenly flung up into the air. Just when Idi 1 was about to fall, he levitated above the ground. He was suddenly pushed toward a large tree behind him.

Idi 1 flicked his wrist and a gush of air pushed him to the side so he wouldn't hit the tree.

A strand of air grabbed Idi's leg and he got flung into a tree. Idi 1 groaned as he looked up at his other self.

"My turn." Idi 1 groaned. He shot toward Idi 2 and pushed him back with the force of the wind. Idi 1 swiped Idi 2's legs and all the air was sucked out of Idi 2 before he disappeared.

. . .

Kathy 1 and Kathy 2 clashed swords. They were battling like gladiators who were able to switch weapons with just their thoughts.

Kathy 2 suddenly changed her weapon to a gun. She spun around and started shooting at Kathy 1. A barrier formed between them, which protected Kathy 1. A gun formed in her hand and she started shooting at her other self. Kathy 1 quickly hid behind a tree as the barrier disappeared.

She took a quick peek only to see a bullet zooming toward her. Kathy 1 stepped to the side and a frisbee formed in her hand. She threw the frisbee which hit Kathy 2's leg. When Kathy 2 lost her balance, Kathy 1 punched her. The force of her punch caused Kathy 2 to disappear.

. . .

Sam 2 screamed as he kicked Sam 1 in the face. Sam 1 spun in the air three times before hitting the cold grass.

"I am starting to think that my power isn't martial arts." he groaned. Sam 2 flipped in the air and brought his foot down on Sam 1, who then rolled over and tried to backhand his other self. Sam 2 blocked the attack, gripped Sam 1's arm, then smacked him in the face.

"Ow." Sam 1 grunted before he was kicked hard in the chest. He flew back and hit a tree.

Sam 2 pushed Sam back into the tree and started rapidly punching him. With each punch, there was a loud THUD as the back of Sam 1's head hit the tree.

His friends watched with concern.

"He's getting killed!" Idi said.

"Be quiet! I'm watching the show! Where did you put the popcorn?" Dany asked. Idi and Kathy glared at him.

"Now is not the time to joke!"

"Sorry." Dany stayed quiet.

"Sam! You got this." Idi cried.

"Thank you!" Sam 2 said.

"No, the other one!"

"Oh." Sam 2 frowned.

"Sam! Fight back!" said Kathy.

"I can't! Oof!" Sam's face hit the tree again. "I'm not strong enough! Ugh! I—Oof!"

"Sam! You beat Steve and **Blade**! And they are like crazy fighters. What makes him so different?" Dany asked.

"Because he is me!"

"Then that is good! He is a reflection of what you can do!"

As Sam 2 kept punching him, Sam 1 thought about what Dany had said. Dany was right: Sam 2 is just a reflection of what *he* can do.

Sam 1 glared at Sam 2. "My turn."

He pushed Sam 2's hand to the side, aggressively punched him in the face multiple times, then spun around in the air and kicked Sam 2 in the face. Sam 2 flew back but rolled over and stood up. The original Sam got ready to do a technique that he had made up himself called Four Shield.

Sam 2 charged toward him, spun in the air, and tried to wheel kick him in the face, but Sam 1 blocked the attack with his forearm. Sam 2 tried to backhand him in the face, but Sam 1 used his other hand to block it. Sam 1 spun around, kicked Sam 2 in the face, and slammed his palm into his chest. Sam 2 stumbled backward, gasped, then disappeared.

Chapter 17

"Oh, my baby." Aleem walked up to Sam and grabbed his arms. "What happened to you? You're bleeding and all bruised up."

Sam had just arrived home. He quickly made something up to make sure his mom did not get worried.

"Um… well, you see I was walking with my friends, but there was like this really unstable bridge and I fell."

"Oh, my baby." His mom said again, "Let me give you some ice packs."

"Mom, I'm fine."

"No, you…" Aleem faltered. A second ago, Sam's face was all bruised up and bloody but now… there was no evidence of any bruises or blood.

"What? How?" Aleem gasped.

"What happened?" Abdul walked into the room.

"Our son came home with bruises and cuts, but now look at him. He is fine!" Aleem explained.

"Great, problem solved then." Abdul shrugged carelessly and walked away. Aleem looked at Sam. She knew something was going on. She put her hand on his face and smiled. "My baby is growing up so quickly…too quickly."

Sam grabbed her hands. "Mom, I'm fine. Don't worry." He smiled and went to his room. He walked toward the window and looked outside at the plants and grass.

"Spill it." someone said behind him. Sam jumped in surprise and turned around to find Yasmin standing in front of his door with her arms crossed.

"What are you doing in my room?" Sam asked.

"I'm your older sister. I can come into your room whenever." Yasmin sat on his tiny twin bed.

"Why are you here? Don't you have to study?"

"It's the weekend. I don't have work... Well, not a lot of it. But first I want you to tell me what is going on."

"Nothing is going on. Why do you ask?"

"Stop lying to me. I know something is going on with you. Suddenly you are strong, tall, and you have sharp eyesight." Yasmin stood up and walked toward him. "So, look me in the eye and tell me what is going on with you."

Sam looked into his sister's emerald eyes. They demanded the truth. Sam grimaced and shook his head. He did not want to tell her.

"Tell me." she demanded. Sam could not hold it any longer.

"I have powers." he blurted out, then he placed his hands over his mouth.

"What?"

"I have powers," he said again. Yasmin glared at him.

"Really? Powers? Is that the best you could come up with?" She laughed. "Oh, well. I don't believe you. But I will find out what is going on and when I do…" she shrugged and walked out of his room. Sam sighed and sat down on his bed.

"That was close."

Chapter 18

On Monday morning, Kathy found the boys walking toward their first period.

Kathy ran up to them. "Guys, you will not believe what I just found out." she said.

"What?" Idi asked.

"You know how we thought that everyone in our class got powers?"

"I thought that?" Dany asked himself.

"I didn't." Idi admitted.

"Yeah, I was so focused on *us* that I forgot about everyone else." Sam shrugged.

Kathy frowned. "Really? Do you boys think about nothing?"

Dany scoffed. "I think about things! I think about the food I am going to eat, the movies I want to watch, my nap times, and… yeah, that is basically it."

Kathy sighed. "Anyway, I *thought* that everyone in Ms. Cortez's first period class got powers, but I was wrong. Turns out, only a few students in each of Ms. Cortez's classes got powers. Not everyone."

"And the Emperors are one of them. So, how do you know this?" asked Idi.

"She just genuinely knows things about people." Sam smiled

Kathy also smiled. "Yeah, that's it…well, I've been keeping an eye on everyone and not a lot of them have powers." Kathy said as they entered their classroom and sat down at their table.

"Good morning, class." Ms. Cortez called.

"Good morning, Ms. Cortez." the class said in unison.

"Wonderful. Anyway, before we start class, I have an announcement to make. This Thursday, the *chosen* students in my class will visit the National Science Museum in Washington D.C.!"

"What do you mean by chosen?" a student asked.

"The plan was at first to take every single student from my classes, but Mr. Xavier said it would be too expensive. But he has provided a plane for a specific number of students!"

"So, who is going?" Idi asked.

"I will pass out the sheets to the chosen students right now!" Ms. Cortez walked to her desk, pulled out a small pile of paper, and passed the sheets out to specific students from each table group.

"You each have been doing very well in class- Dany, you could use some improvement though- so you all will be able to go." she said as she passed out papers to everyone at their table.

Kathy read through the paper. There was a long paragraph about where they were going, what they were seeing, and why they were going. At the bottom, it asked for the student's signature and the parent's signature.

When she was done, Kathy shuddered. She was going back to America, after nearly a year. Because of the gun violence and COVID-19, her parents decided it was best to move to Canada. Canada came with its own set of struggles but here she felt more... free.

Kathy sighed and closed her eyes, remembering everything.

Chapter 19

Later that week, Sam and his friends were driven to the airport by Idi's parents. It was the first time they had ever been in the same car together, so it was quite exciting.

Idi's dad, Kwame, was very nice and he looked exactly like Idi but with a thick beard.

"So, Sam, how do you like XMS?" Kwame asked.

"It's pretty good. I got my friends with me so that is all I need." Sam answered. Kwame smiled and continued driving.

Dany was shaking with excitement. "Wow! I can't believe we're going to America together!"

"I know! So exciting!" Idi cried out. "Dad, it's almost 8:00, the plane leaves at 8:50."

"We're almost there. Don't worry."

Five minutes later, they arrived at the Xavier Airport, which was the size of a football stadium. Mr. Xavier owned the airport and trained most of the greatest pilots in the world here. There was an X symbol on top of the airport, but unlike XMS, the X was created by two planes that were crossed together.

There was a small garage that Ms. Cortez had told them to park in, so that is what they did. They parked inside the garage, walked out of the car, and took their bags and suitcases out of the trunk. Ms. Cortez spotted them and walked over to greet them.

"Oh, Mr. Bocku! Nice to meet you! So, is there anything that I need to know about Idi before we leave?"

"No." Kwame answered.

"Great! We are just waiting on some other parents, but we are departing soon, so it is best to say your goodbyes now."

Kwame nodded and turned around. "Be good guys. Okay?"

"Yes." Kathy, Idi, and Sam said in unison.

"Sir, yes, sir!" Dany saluted. Kwame chuckled and ruffled his son's hair before getting in his car and driving away.

"Isn't it kind of weird that parents aren't allowed?" Sam asked.

"Oh yeah, it's a new policy. Parents can't come because some students are embarrassed to have their parents there." Kathy answered.

"There were a lot of complaints last year about it. So, the school board decided on a NO PARENTS policy." Idi added in. Ten minutes later, every student who had been chosen came in.

"Well, looks like we're all here! Is everyone ready?" Ms. Cortez asked the crowd. Some said "Yeah," while others said "Meh, my parents made me."

The garage door opened, revealing the runway which stretched out long and far. On the runway was a blue colored plane with an X on the rudder. There was a large staircase that led to the inside of the plane. A man in a pilot suit stepped out of the plane and walked toward them all. The man was tall and had a red mustache, barely any hair, and a long nose.

"Hello, my name is Captain Elken. Welcome to Xavier Airlines." Captain Elken announced. "You see, this plane isn't like normal planes. This plane is the first fully electric plane that Mr. Xavier built himself. What a genius he is! Anyway, it has everything a plane has except for more tech and a large generator in the middle."

"Isn't that wonderful, students? You are all going to be the first to experience a flight in the first electric plane!" All the students clapped. Sam looked through the crowd and then frowned. Only a few feet away from them stood the Emperors. Sam told his friends and they frowned.

"Let's just ignore them." Kathy suggested. After that, they all boarded the plane, which was very modern. The walls were patterned with blue and yellow lines. The seats were very comfortable and there was a large tablet for each passenger. There were two aisles which were split between a row of seats.

Sam and his friends sat in the same row. They put their bags in the overhead bins and sat down.

"Well, this will be fun." Dany said.

"Yeah, nothing will go wrong." Idi said. But he was wrong.

Chapter 20

A while later, the plane sped down the runway and they were off into the sky. Sam had only been in one plane before and that was the military plane that helped him and his family flee from Afghanistan. At least in this plane, he was with friends and not soldiers.

The first thing Dany did was watch a movie on the large tablet that was provided for them. Idi took a nap and Kathy just sat there, thinking.

Sam was sitting by the window, so he gazed out at the scenery. Below, he could see the snowy city of Toronto. It got smaller and smaller as they flew higher and higher. When they passed the white clouds, the city disappeared from his sight.

Sam decided that he should do something or else he was going to get bored. He read a couple of chapters of his book, then he watched a movie that he had never seen before, and then he closed his eyes and took a long nap.

. . .

A couple of hours later, Sam learned that they were just above Maryland. There was only an hour left before they reached their destination.

Sam had to go to the restroom and he was going to ask his friends if they could let him pass but decided to use his new strength instead. He grabbed the small air condition unit, pulled himself up, squeezed his legs into the aisle, and then jumped. During all this, Kathy was watching him in confusion.

When he was on the aisle, Sam sighed and walked toward the bathroom at the end of the aisle. He walked until he finally reached the restroom, which was hidden behind a long silky curtain. To his disappointment, the bathroom was being used.

He turned around and gasped. Standing in front of him was Steve Xavier.

"Well, well, well, look at what I have here." the bully smirked.

"Steve, what do you want?" Sam asked.

"You humiliated me! Now my father is very disappointed and the only thing that I can do about it is kill you!"

Steve's hand shifted into a blade and Sam gasped. The bully swung his hand-blade toward his face and Sam quickly moved out of the way and started running away. Steve's blade cut through the bathroom door, revealing a kid sitting on the toilet seat with his pants down. The kid shrieked and pulled his pants up. Steve barely noticed and he started chasing after Sam, who was running down the aisle as quickly as he could.

Bill and Nill saw Sam running and they jumped out of their seats. Suddenly, Idi jumped out of his seat and blasted Bill and Nill with the wind. They flew to the other aisle and smashed into a window. The kids who were sitting in the seats that the twins crashed onto screamed.

"Sam, what is going on?" Idi asked.

"Steve is trying to kill me!" Sam watched as Steve toward them ran down the aisle

"Again?!" Dany and Kathy both stood up.

"Yeah!"

Bill and Nill had both recovered and were now standing up. Bill's hands glowed with magma and Nill's hands glowed with electricity.

"We'll take them on. Together!" said Idi.

"Okay, but we have to keep everyone else safe!" Sam said. "Steve wants me! I'll draw him away-"

"I'll come with you!" Kathy insisted.

Sam nodded. "You guys take care of Bill and Nill."

Sam and Kathy ran off. Steve pushed Dany and Idi to the side and chased after their friends.

"Ready?" Idi asked.

"Always." Dany grinned. Suddenly, electricity buzzed around Nill and it raised him into the air. Dany ran off using his super-speed with Nill chasing after him. Bill started shooting magma balls at Idi who used the air to cool them down.

"Hey, guys! It's Tony, coming to you live from a plane!" a boy named Tony said behind Idi.

Tony was live streaming a video that was recording all the action. "Right now, this kid over here is like– Hey!"

Idi had slapped the phone from his hand. "Don't make a video."

"Look out!" Tony screamed. Idi turned around to find a large ball of magma shooting toward him. Before he could react, Tony reached out and suddenly a purple orb formed around the magma. Tony gasped in shock and the orb disappeared.

The magma ball hit the plane's wall and a large chunk of the wall melted. The cold air flew in and multiple kids screamed as they were pulled from their seats.

"No!" Idi swung his arms and the wind subsided, which caused multiple kids to fall back into their seats. Idi sighed with relief, but then Bill pushed him to the ground.

"Time to melt!" Bill screamed. His hand glowed with magma and he tried to touch Idi's face. Idi struggled to protect himself.

· · ·

Near the front of the plane, Sam and Kathy were running for their life. Steve swung his hand-blades, which they had to constantly dodge.

"I'm tired of this!" Kathy exclaimed. She spun around and summoned a sword. She and Steve exchanged multiple attacks, but Kathy was weaker than Steve. She was pushed to the side and nearly knocked unconscious. Steve kept chasing after Sam.

. . .

In the middle of the plane, Dany was constantly dodging the electricity bolts that Nill kept shooting at him.

"Come on. You know I am too quick for you." Dany said. Nill screamed with so much rage that electricity bolts rained down all around them. Dany quickly ran around and shielded multiple students from getting hit.

"What is going on?!" Ms. Cortez asked.

"No time to explain!" Dany said. He was suddenly hit with a bolt of electricity. He smashed into small seats and fell to the floor. Nill raised his glowing fist and brought it down. Dany quickly moved to the side and Nill's fist broke through the floor. Because the battery of the plane was in the middle of it, the electricity from Nill's fist caused the battery to overload and then…

The entire plane shut down. The light, the power, the controls, everything turned off. All the students started screaming in panic.

And then the plane started falling.

. . .

The plane jerked forward and Sam slid to the ground. Steve raised his hand-blade, but because of the sudden jerk of the plane he stumbled clumsily forward. Sam spread his legs out and Steve's hand-blade stabbed through the ground, where Sam's legs had been. He bent his legs and kicked Steve in the face, which caused him to stumble backward.

I have to get to the cockpit, Sam thought. He stood up and started running but Steve grabbed his shoulder and threw him back. Steve stood menacingly in front of him, blocking his way forward.

"You aren't getting to the cockpit." Steve growled. As the plane rapidly shook, Sam watched all the other students crying and screaming in terror panic.

"Guess I am going to have to improvise then." Sam opened the nearest exit door and a cold gush of air flew in. He jumped out of the plane, swung himself around, and grabbed the outside of a window. He kicked the door closed just as Steve was about to jump out.

Steve pushed his hand-blade through the window and Sam quickly pushed himself back. He grabbed the blade and used it to slide on the roof of the plane. Then he started running to the front.

Suddenly, Steve broke through the roof and raised his new weapon that had formed. It was curved and long like a scythe. Steve brought his hand-scythe down and Sam quickly moved out of the way. Steve's other hand turned into scythe and he kept attacking Sam.

Just as the scythe was about to hit his face, he flipped back onto his hands and the scythe sailed over his body. Sam flipped back onto his legs as Steve brought his hand-scythe down again, which Sam dodged. The scythe broke through the roof and Sam ran up Steve's arm, jumped, and kneed him in the face. Steve groaned and fell on back, unconscious.

Sam ran to the front of the plane, slid to the side (the speed of the plane helped him slide faster), grabbed the window, and jumped into the cockpit.

The pilots had been electrocuted and they were slumped in their seats, unconscious. Sam pushed one of the pilots out of their seats and grabbed the yoke. Because he did not know how to operate a plane, Sam started pressing random buttons, but they did nothing due to the lack of power. Sam tried pulling the yoke, but it did nothing to change the plane's course.

Kathy, who had recovered, ran into the cockpit and studied their situation.

"Nothing's working!" Sam cried out. "What do we do?"

"I don't know!" said Kathy. Suddenly, Steve's blade broke through the ceiling of the cockpit. It circled around and then… The cockpit broke off.

Sam was pulled away by Steve who had fallen off the roof and was now grabbing Sam's leg to keep him from flying away. Kathy had summoned a rope which was tied to one of the unoccupied seats. While holding onto the rope, she was tightly grabbing Sam's hand.

"Let me go!" Sam screamed.

"No!"

"Kathy! You have to!"

Kathy shook her head. "I'm not letting you go! You'll die!"

"Kathy…" Sam said calmly. She looked at Sam with tears in her eyes.

"Steve wants me. No one else. I can't put anyone else in danger. It'll be okay… I promise."

Kathy closed her eyes, took a deep breath, and loosened her grip. She felt Sam's hand leave hers and he flew away. A few moments later, Kathy opened her eyes and wiped the tears from her face. She could see the large buildings of Maryland getting closer to them.

"I have to protect them." she said.

Chapter 21

Inside the plane, Idi was still being pushed to the ground with Bill trying to melt his face.

While this was happening, multiple students were screaming in horror as the plane nosedived.

Idi looked out the window and saw two silhouettes falling through the sky: Sam and Steve.

Idi groaned and blasted Bill into the roof. He rolled to the side just as Bill landed and, once again, he blasted him away. Bill crashed into the overhead bin and he was knocked unconscious. Idi sighed with relief and ran off to find Dany, who was dodging all of Nill's attacks and protecting students at the same time.

Unfortunately, one of the students got electrocuted and passed out. Dany gasped in horror and he quickly ran, his anger fueling him, toward Nill and elbowed him in the chest. Nill gasped as all the air was sucked of him, and he fell to the ground unconscious.

"Great job." Idi said as he met up with Dany.

"Thanks."

"Boys." Kathy, who was bending over from the ceiling, said as she knocked on a window. "I could use a little bit of help up here."

Moments later, the boys met Kathy on the roof of the plane.

"What's our situation?" Dany asked.

"Well, we have a lot of problems. The worst being that we're headed toward that city with hundreds, maybe thousands, of people, including everyone on this plane." Kathy explained. "Also, Sam is fighting Steve somewhere over there and the plane is on the brink of breaking down."

"So, what do we do?" Idi asked.

"I have a plan. Idi, you have to make sure this plane doesn't break down. I'll control the plane and try my best to steer it toward that large field. Dany, when we're close enough, you have to go and save those people in that building." Kathy pointed toward one of the large buildings that was near the field that they were going to crash on.

"How am I supposed to get there?" Dany asked. Kathy whispered the answer into his ear. Dany frowned but then smiled.

"Risky, but heroic-y." he said.

"What about Sam?" Idi asked.

"We'll save him first while we're on our way down." Kathy told them. "You guys ready?"

"Ready." Idi and Dany said in unison.

Kathy nodded and she summoned two long ropes. She lassoed them to the wings of the plane, which allowed her to take control. Behind her, Idi swung his arms around. Large waves of air spun around the plane.

Idi made a gesture as if he was pulling on an invisible lever. Suddenly, there was a large creak, and Dany felt parts of the plane come together as if it was being squeezed. Dany ran inside the plane.

"It's so cold in this world!" a student screamed.

"We're all going to die!" another screamed.

"Everyone keep calm!" Dany screamed over their cries. "Stay in your seats! And don't get out, whatsoever! Everything is going to be fine!"

All the students and Ms. Cortez nodded and they clenched their seats so tightly that their fingers became completely white. Dany nodded and he jumped back onto the roof.

· · ·

While his friends were trying to control the plane, Sam was falling at a rapid speed and at the same time he was trying not to get killed.
Steve kept swinging his hand-blades at Sam, who had to keep dodging. He kicked Steve with his legs and they got separated. The world spun around him in circles as he fell through the cold and wispy air. He controlled himself by spreading his arms and legs out.

Suddenly, Steve tackled Sam and aimed his blade at Sam's face. Sam blocked the attack with his forearm and struggled to keep control.

"Stop!" Sam yelled through the screaming cold wind.

"No!" Steve pushed harder but Sam held the blade in place.

"Steve, look, I know that you hate me, but our rivalry doesn't have to be so bad that it causes other people's lives to be in danger! Stop now! If you don't then a lot of people are going to get hurt… maybe even killed!" Upon hearing this, Steve's eyes widened. He stayed quiet for a few moments, lost in thought.

"Oh my god! What have I done?!" he screamed. Steve shook his head, disappointed by his own foolishness. "I am so sorry, Sam. My rage blinded me from seeing what I was doing to other people. I am sorry. I'll explain everything later." Sam nodded and he let go of Steve. They both slowly glided toward the city.

They got closer and closer to the city while the broken plane flew closer and closer to them. Right when they were only about 50 feet away from a large building… They got sucked into the plane.

Sam and Steve were both tossed around in the plane. They hit multiple seats and walls as students screamed in surprise. Sam groaned on the ground as his face exploded with pain.

"Here." Steve had already stood up and was now reaching out to help Sam. He grabbed his hand and stood up. They jumped through the large cuts in the ceiling and landed in front of Dany.

"Evil person! Evil person!" Dany cried out, pointing at Steve.

"Dany, he's not evil!" Sam jumped between them, trying to calm Dany down. Dany paused and studied Sam's facial expression. He was telling the truth.

Dany sighed. "Fine."

"Dany! It's time!" Kathy called. Dany walked next to Kathy and he watched as they got closer to the buildings.

"Idi! Now!" Kathy screamed. Air whirled around Dany and he was suddenly pushed toward the largest building in the city. He flung his arms and legs in the air and laughed.

"I'm the king of the world!" he howled before he crashed through the building's window on one of the top floors. He hit a desk, flipped over, and landed hard on the soft ground.

Dany groaned in pain, then stood up.

"Are you okay?" a lady in a suit walked up to him.

"I'm fine. But you guys are not because that plane is coming here quickly. But don't worry, I'll get you guys out of here!"

A businessman in a suit stood up. "How? You are just a kid!"

Dany grinned and used his super-speed to run around the room as fast as he possibly could. He gathered all the workers, then he ran down the building's staircase, dragging the workers along with him. In no time, he made it to the first floor. He ran out of the building, ran a couple of blocks away from it, and placed the workers in front of a restaurant.

"I'll be back." Dany ran back to the building and did the same thing for each floor. Five minutes later, when the plane was only a couple of feet away from the building, Dany managed to grab everyone in the building and move them to safety.

"Is everyone okay?" Dany asked. "And is everyone here?"

"Yes." most of the businessmen and women said.

"No!" a woman screamed. "My son! He's still in the building! On the top level!"

"Why is your son in the building?!"

"It's Take-Your-Child-to-Work-Day!"

Dany groaned. "Americans."

He hurried back to the building. He ran up the stairs to the last floor. He looked around the room and saw a little boy on the floor in a corner, hugging his knees and shaking with fear. Dany looked at the window and saw that the plane was only a few yards away. He quickly jumped over multiple desks, slid on file cabinets, and hurdled over chairs. He reached the other side of the room, grabbed the little boy, and ran for his life. He sprinted down the staircase, out of the building, and went to the site where he had placed all the workers.

"Here you go, ma'am." Dany said as he gave the boy to his mother.

"Thank you, so much!" She cried tears of happiness as she embraced her son.

Dany turned around and watched as the left wing of the plane cut through the roof of the building, causing the top of the building to rip apart into pieces. The left wing of the plane was ripped away as it collided with the building, leaving only the right wing.

. . .

When the left wing fell apart, Kathy lost her grip on the ropes and she flew back. Sam managed to save her, but now no one was controlling the right wing!

Steve lunged after the rope that controlled the right wing, grabbed it, and pulled with all his might. The plane tilted and turned toward the large field. Steve stopped pulling and the plane zoomed toward the field.

"Everyone hold on!" Steve screamed.

Sam and Kathy grabbed the rudder. Idi continued controlling the wind for as long as he could as he braced for impact. Then the plane crashed with a large BUMP!

Trees were pushed down under the weight of the plane and the grass was ripped apart, causing the plane to leave a trail of dirt behind it. Sam and Kathy fell off the plane and toppled onto the dirt. Steve and Idi stumbled but they managed to stay on the roof. Then the plane came to an abrupt stop.

There was silence for a few moments but it was interrupted when the plane creaked and broke down. The rudder and the right wing fell apart and the windows were shattered.

Sam ran inside the plane and looked at the mess. Bags and other belongings were all over the floor. Steam hissed from broken electronics. It was as if a group of soldiers had stormed the place.

"Is everyone okay?" Sam asked. The students and Ms. Cortez were too frightened to speak but they all nodded. Sam sighed and fell on the nearest unoccupied seat. They had managed to save everyone.

Chapter 22

Later that night, a large number of police, ambulances, and news crews came to the plane wreckage. The ambulance took the injured (not many were injured, thankfully) to the hospital.

A group of police inspected the plane while another group questioned the students and Ms. Cortez while reporters took notes of their responses. Everyone said that the plane lost its power and it suddenly started falling and that they knew nothing more. Obviously, Sam, his friends, and the Emperors knew more, but they did not want to seem suspicious.

XMS was contacted and Mr. Xavier said that a hotel and transportation would be provided for them and the class would leave tomorrow.

Because it was such a cold night, the students were given hot chocolate and warm blankets. Sam watched as students were transported to the hotel they were staying at. He then saw Steve sitting alone on a nearby bench, drinking hot chocolate. He walked over to Steve and sat down.

"Hey."

"Hey." Steve said quietly. His face was shrouded in shadow. "It's time I explain things, I guess." Sam nodded.

"Ok," Steve took a deep breath. "You may not believe me when I say this but… I am Mr. Xavier's son. My last name is Xavier, you know?"

Sam's eyes widened in shock. "I thought that was a coincidence. I didn't expect you to be related to Mr. Xavier!"

"Because I am a bully who doesn't like education, unlike my father who is a billionaire who loves education?"

Sam grimaced in embarrassment. "Um… yes."

"I understand. But you know, I never wanted to be a bully. You see, at first I loved learning, but I loved playing football—American Football— more!"

"You like playing football?"

"Yeah, I just play in secret. Anyway, I've always wanted to grow up and be the best football player of all time! Even better than Tom Brady! But my father said no and that football was another version of violence because, you know, tackling and stuff. So whenever I'm around him, I have to be reading or doing something educational. If I am playing a sport, then he gets mad at me."

"But don't we have to play sports at school?"

"That's a policy. But when I am not at school, I have to do what he says."

"So, you decided to be a bully?"

"If my father isn't going to let me live my dream of being a football player, then why should I follow his dream of giving people education?"

Sam considered it for a second and tilted his head. He looked at Steve, who was staring off into the distance, lost in thought. Sam suddenly felt bad for him. All he wanted to do was become an American Football player, but his father was not letting him.

On the brochure of XMS, it was said that XMS helped you fulfill your dreams. Steve's story proved that to be wrong, even though he was Mr. Xavier's son.

"Steve," He said, "You should tell your father you want to be a football player."

"I do. He doesn't listen."

"Then make him listen. Look, I don't know your dad, but I can tell he's very strict. What I do know is that if he doesn't listen to his son's dreams, then he is the worst father in the world. You might as well just run away!"

Steve sighed. "My father isn't who he is for no reason. When I was little, he was a nice dude! He laughed, he played, he took me to the movies…" he smiled. "It was great. But after my mom died, it took a toll on him. He didn't eat or sleep. He was always upstairs in his office, day and night. And he wouldn't even look at me because he said that he couldn't look at me without thinking about my mom." When Steve said this, he brushed a lock of his blond hair from his face. "It made me feel like… with my mom dead and my dad avoiding me, I didn't have parents at all. I felt like an orphan." Steve paused, then looked at Sam and smiled. "But I am going to make him do what my mom always did: listen."

Sam and Steve smiled and shook each other's hand.

Chapter 23

The next day, the class took the afternoon flight back to Canada. In a couple of hours, they reached Toronto. The children were met with warm hugs and kisses from their parents. An hour later, Mr. Xavier announced that Ms. Cortez's classes would have the week off so they could get some rest. Sam's wounds healed in about a day and he was full of energy two days later.

Every day during the evening, Sam would meet his friends at the park. His friends were still so shocked that they had managed to save their class and civilians.

"Did you guys see how I saved all those civilians in that building?! No human could have possibly done that!" Dany cried out joyfully.

Kathy scoffed. "Who was the one controlling the plane so we wouldn't all die?!"

"Who was the one holding the plane together so we wouldn't all fall to our deaths?" Idi asked. Their conversations went on like this every day.

On the last day of break, Sam was looking through his emails when he saw an email from Steve. Sam opened it and read through it.

Dear Sam,

I just want to thank you for helping me. I told my dad what I wanted to do and he listened this time. There was quite a lot of protesting, but in the end he agreed with me and he put me in the Toronto American Football Group! My first day will be March 1st! Anyway, I also wanted to tell you that Bill, Nill, and I are no longer doing the bullying thing. The Emperors are no more! Thank you for changing my life, Sam.

Sincerely,
Steve Xavier

    When Sam was done reading, he smiled. *People can change*, he thought.

    He looked at the time, put his jacket and shoes on, and walked to the park to see his friends sitting where they usually sat.

    "Hey, Sam!" his friends said in unison.

    "Hi, guys!" Sam sat on the bench with them.

    "I just realized, we need a team name," Dany said.

    "Ooh, how about The Fearsome 4?!" Idi asked.

    "Nope! How about The Fantastic 4?!" Dany asked.

    "Taken." Kathy pointed out. All three of them kept coming up with names that all sounded horrible and half of them were already taken.

    "How about K.I.D.S.?" Sam blurted out.

"Kids? What type of name is that? It's already obvious we're kids!" Dany whined.

"No, not that type of kids! K.I.D.S.!" Sam pointed at Kathy "K," he pointed at Idi "I," he pointed at Dany "D," he pointed at himself "S. K.I.D.S.!"

"Oh." Idi and Kathy said in unison.

"I like it." Idi said.

"Me too." said Kathy.

"I think we should still go with Fantastic 4." Dany admitted with a shrug. Sam, Kathy, and Idi all glared at Dany.

"Fine, we can go with K.I.D.S." he groaned. The team smiled. K.I.D.S. was their official team name!

"So, who wants to go take down some bad guys in the city?" Kathy asked.

"Nah, too tired." Dany yawned.

"How could you be tired?!"

"What? We just saved hundreds of people in a moving plane!"

"That was a week ago!"

"So?" Dany raised his eyebrow
"*Superheroes* need their rest, don't they?"

Epilogue

Blade sat in his room. He had purposely turned the lights off and kept the fan on so that it would give the room an eerie feeling. The only light came from the computer that he was sitting in front of. Blade was waiting for a very important message that could change civilization itself.

Suddenly, there was a DING and a message popped up. He clicked the message and it opened a video. The person who was making the video was his friend, Jackson.

"Blade!" Jackson said in the video. "You will not believe what is happening. Me and a bunch of other students are on this plane to get to Washington D.C. but suddenly these kids with glowing magma and electricity started attacking these other kids who can control the air and run super fast! But the strangest thing of all is this..." The video shifted to the roof of the plane where it showed Sam fighting Steve.

Blade paused the video there and opened the Emergency Call on his computer. He dialed 911 and a second later the call was picked up.

"Hello, this is 911, what is your emergency?" a female voice asked.

"Ma'am this is not *my* emergency, this is the world's emergency." Blade said.

"What do you mean?"

"This is hard to believe, but there is a group of kids who have powers or special abilities. And if their powers grow to a certain level, then they will be the biggest threat the world has ever seen. And I want to stop them."

Our favorite team of superheroes will return in Book 2 of the trilogy!

K.I.D.S.
Revelation

Aydin Rizqi is a young author and currently resides in California. He has been writing and telling stories since he was 7 years old, and has self-published many books. He is inspired by Rick Riordan and J.K Rowling. As a young author, he is still learning about the publishing world but receives a tremendous amount of support from his friends and family.